P9-DCJ-203

For Tara, wearer of adorable hats, who wooed me with handmade valentines.
Cara mia, I still have a crush on you!

Also for Melissa, Isabel, Benji and Brian, Jodi and Ro, David, Annie, Melody, Chelsea,
Sandy, and everyone at Thrive Youth Center. For all of us who have longed for a story of
our own. Love, Charlotte

For J. N. and H. Y., even though you'll never know —C. C.

Farrar Straus Giroux Books for Young Readers • An imprint of Macmillan Publishing Group, LLC • 120 Broadway, New York, NY 10271 • mackids.com • Text copyright © 2021 by Charlotte Sullivan Wild • Pictures copyright © 2021 by Charlene Chua • All rights reserved. Our books may be purchased in bulk for promotional, educational, or business use. Please contact your local bookseller or the Macmillan Corporate and Premium Sales Department at (800) 221-7945 ext. 5442 or by email at MacmillanSpecialMarkets@macmillan.com. Library of Congress Cataloging-in-Publication Data is available. • First edition, 2021 • Book design by Aram Kim • Color separations by Bright Arts (H.K.) Ltd. • Printed in China by RR Donnelley Asia Printing Solutions Ltd., Dongguan City, Guangdong Province • ISBN 978-0-374-31372-2 (hardcover) • 10 9 8 7 6 5 4 3 2 1

Love, Violet

Words by Charlotte Sullivan Wild   *Pictures by* Charlene Chua

Farrar Straus Giroux

New York

As far as Violet was concerned,
only one person in her class raced like the wind.
Only one had a leaping laugh.
Only one made Violet's heart skip.

Mira.

Every day, Violet dreamed

of astounding Mira with heroic feats

and bringing her treasures

and galloping off together on adventures!

But whenever Mira came near . . .

"What are you drawing, Violet?"

"Want to play horses, Violet?"

"Where's Violet? We're line buddies today."

. . . Violet went shy.

One wintry day, Violet had an idea.

An idea with crayons and
scissors, glitter and glue.

When it was just right,
she signed her valentine,
Love, Violet.

Maybe tomorrow their
adventures would begin!

On Valentine's Day, Violet woke to shimmering snow.

On went her boots and lucky cowgirl hat.

And under that hat went Violet's surprise!

As Violet kicked through snow to school,
Carlos asked, "Did everybody bring valentines?"
"I bet you made a SPECIAL one for somebody!"
teased Jade.
"Ewww! Did not!" cried Carlos. "Violet, did YOU?"
Violet blushed hot. "I gotta go." She darted through
the wintry gust with her hat pulled low.

Just then, Mira raced up like the wind.

"Nice hat, Violet."

Snow sparkled on Mira's eyelashes.

Mira was magnificent.

But what if Violet's valentine *wasn't*?

Suddenly, Violet's heart thundered like a
hundred galloping horses.

She reached for her hat and . . .

THUMPity, THUMPity, THUMPity!

bolted.

All day long, Violet's stomach lurched.

What if Violet couldn't give her valentine?

What if Mira didn't *want* her valentine?

What if . . . they never adventured?

"Time for valentines!" called Mr. York.
Violet squeaked.

Queasy and quivering, Violet delivered her valentines.

All. But. One.

She looked left.

She looked right.

She lifted her hat . . .

THUMPity! THUMPity! THUMP—

"Did you give all your valentines?" Mira asked, appearing out of nowhere.

Violet jumped! She smacked right into Mira and tumbled into the coats.

All around her, kids hooted and howled.

Violet shrank into the tangle of scarves.

She wanted to say sorry.

She wanted to give Mira her valentine.

Instead, she scrambled away,
hiding her eyes (and her surprise)
under her hat.

At recess, Violet made a lonely angel in the snow.

How could she ever face Mira now?

Then laughter lassoed across the playground.

A laugh like leaping horses.

A laugh that warmed Violet down into her boots.

Violet sprang up.

Only one person had praised her hat.

Only one hadn't laughed when she fell.

Only one had ever asked her to play horses.

Could it be Mira *wanted* to be her valentine?

"MIRA!" cried Violet. "I have something for you!"
Violet flew through the snow.

She scaled drifts!

Slid across ice!

She even dodged a barrage of snowballs
under the jungle gym WHEN—

—the wind **whooOOOSHED** up Violet's hat,
and Mira's valentine twirled down,

down,

down

beneath stampeding feet.

"NOOOOOOO!"

Mira raced like the wind. "Violet! What's wrong?"
Violet sniffed. "This was for you. But it's *ruined*."

"For me? Violet . . . it's so pretty!"
Mira tucked a torn bit into her cap.
It glittered beside her hair.

Then, with a shy smile, Mira reached into her pocket
and pulled out a locket.
"For you," said Mira.

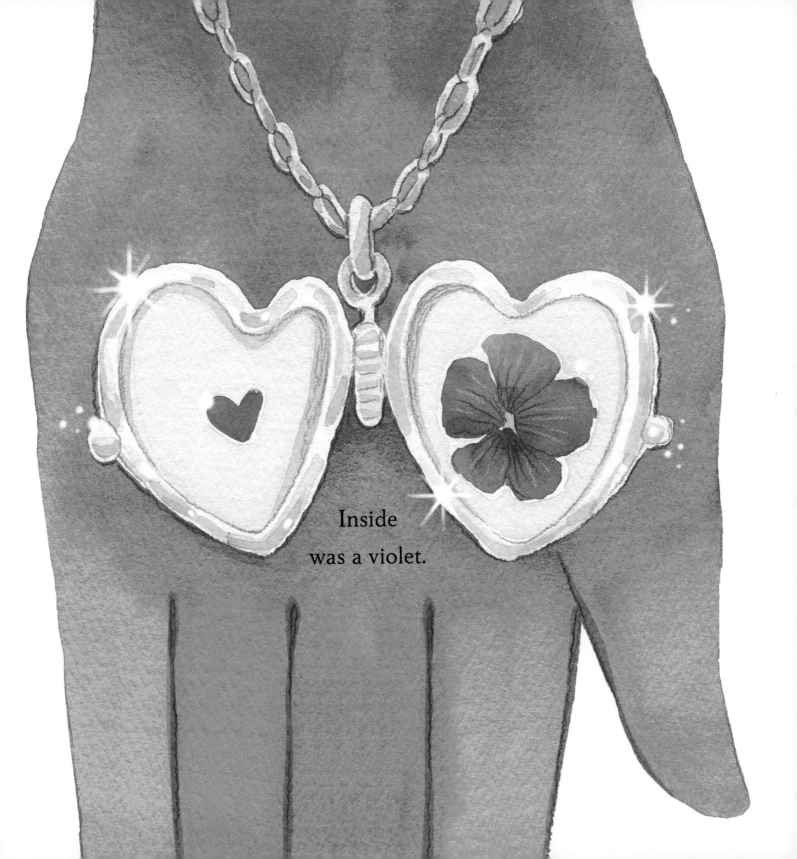

Inside
was a violet.

"Want to go on an adventure?" asked Violet.

"Yes!" cried Mira.

And they were off,
    galloping over snowy drifts
        to see what they might find.

Together.

Author's Note

The creation of this book was supported by a Beyond the Pure Fellowship for Writers grant from Intermedia Arts, made possible, in part, by the support of the Jerome Foundation; a Next Step Fund grant from the Metropolitan Regional Arts Council of the Twin Cities; and the Shabo Award for Children's Picture Book Writers from the Loft Literary Center.

Charlotte Sullivan Wild was a fiscal year 2015 recipient of an Artist Initiative grant from the Minnesota State Arts Board. The creation of this book was supported by the voters of Minnesota through a grant from the Minnesota State Arts Board, thanks to a legislative appropriation from the arts and cultural heritage fund.

MINNESOTA
STATE ARTS BOARD

CLEAN
WATER
LAND &
LEGACY
AMENDMENT

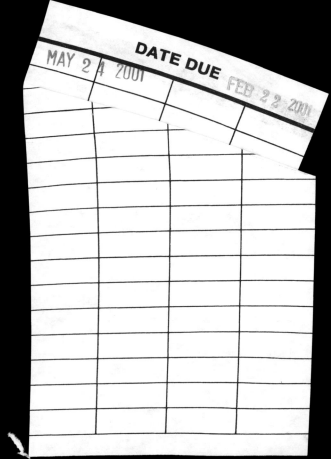

DATE DUE

MAY 2 4 2001   FEB 2 2 2001

DATE DUE